The reproductions in this book have been made using the most modern electronic scanning methods from entirely new transparencies of Cicely Mary Barker's original watercolours. They enable Cicely Mary Barker's skill as an artist to be appreciated as never before.

The original illustration of the Self-Heal Fairy has been lost so a first edition has been used to reproduce this picture.

FREDERICK WARNE

Published by the Penguin Group
Registered office: 80 Strand, London, WC2R ORL
Penguin Young Readers Group, 345 Hudson Street, New York, N.Y. 10014, USA

First published 1948 by Frederick Warne
This edition with new reproductions first published 1990
This edition first published 2007

Manufactured in China

FLOWER
FAIRIES
OF THE
WAYSIDE

❖

CICELY MARY BARKER

Open Your Eyes!

To shop, and school, to work and play,
The busy people pass all day;
They hurry, hurry, to and fro,
And hardly notice as they go
The wayside flowers, known so well,
Whose names so few of them can tell.

They never think of fairy-folk
Who may be hiding for a joke!

O, if these people understood
What's to be found by field and wood;
What fairy secrets are made plain
By any footpath, road, or lane—
They'd go with open eyes, and *look*,
(As you will, when you've read this book)
And then at least they'd learn to see
How pretty common things can be!

The Song of the
Jack-by-the-Hedge Fairy

"'Morning, Sir, and how-d'ye-do?
  'Morning, pretty lady!"
That is Jack saluting you,
  Where the lane is shady.

Don't you know him? Straight and tall—
  Taller than the nettles;
Large and light his leaves; and small
  Are his buds and petals.

Small and white, with petals four,
  See his flowers growing!
If you never knew before,
  There is Jack for knowing!

(Jack-by-the-hedge is also called Garlic Mustard,
and Sauce Alone.)

The Song of the Greater Celandine Fairy

You come with the Spring,
   O swallow on high!
You come with the Spring,
   And so do I.

Your nest, I know,
   Is under the eaves;
While far below
   Are my flowers and leaves.

Yet, to and fro
   As you dart and fly,
You swoop so low
   That you brush me by!

I come with the Spring;
   The wall is my home;
I come with the Spring
   When the swallows come.

(The name "Celandine" comes from the Greek word for "swallow", and this celandine used sometimes to be called "swallow-wort". It has orange-coloured juice in its stems, and is no relation to the Lesser Celandine, which is in *Flower Fairies of the Spring*; but it is a relation of the Horned Poppy, which you will find further on in this book.)

The Song of
the Ground Ivy Fairy

In Spring he is found;
He creeps on the ground;
But someone's to blame
For the rest of his name—
For Ivy he's *not*!
Oh dear, what a lot
Of muddles we make!
It's quite a mistake,
And really a pity
Because he's so pretty;
He deserves a nice name—
Yes, *someone's* to blame!

(But he has some other names, which we do not hear
very often; here are four of them: Robin-run-up-the-
dyke, Runnadyke, Run-away-Jack, Creeping Charlie.)

THE SONG OF
THE RED CAMPION FAIRY

Here's a cheerful somebody,
   By the woodland's edge;
Campion the many-named,
   Robin-in-the-Hedge.

Coming when the bluebells come,
   When they're gone, he stays,
(Round Robin, Red Robin)
   All the summer days.

Soldiers' Buttons, Robin Flower,
   In the lane or wood;
Robin Redbreast, Red Jack,
   Yes, and Robin Hood!

The Song of the Rose-Bay Willow-Herb Fairy

On the breeze my fluff is blown;
So my airy seeds are sown.

Where the earth is burnt and sad,
I will come to make it glad.

All forlorn and ruined places,
All neglected empty spaces,

I can cover—only think!—
With a mass of rosy pink.

Burst then, seed-pods; breezes, blow!
Far and wide my seeds shall go!

(Another name for this Willow-Herb is "Fireweed",
because of its way of growing where there have
been heath or forest fires.)

The Song of the Black Medick Fairies

"Why are we called 'Black', sister,
　　When we've yellow flowers?"
"I will show you why, brother:
　　See these seeds of ours?
Very soon each tiny seed
　　Will be turning black indeed!"

The Song of
the Bee Orchis Fairy

In the grass o' the bank,
  by the side o' the way,
    Where your feet may stray
    On your luckiest day,
There's a sight most rare
  that your eyes may see:
A beautiful orchis that looks like a bee!
A velvety bee, with a proud little elf,
Who looks like the wonderful
  orchis himself—
    In the grass o' the hill,
    Not often, but still
    Just once in a way
    On your luckiest day!

The Song of
the White Bindweed Fairy

O long long stems that twine!
O buds, so neatly furled!
O great white bells of mine,
(None purer in the world)
Each lasting but one day!
O leafy garlands, hung
In wreaths beside the way—
Well may your praise be sung!

(But this Bindweed, which is a big sister to the little pink
Field Convolvulus, is not good to have in gardens,
though it is so beautiful; because it winds around other
plants and trees. One of its names is "Hedge Strangler".
Morning Glories are a garden kind of Convolvulus.)

The Song of the Red Clover Fairy

The Fairy: O, what a great big bee
Has come to visit me!
He's come to find my honey.
O, what a great big bee!

The Bee: O, what a great big Clover!
I'll search it well, all over,
And gather all its honey.
O, what a great big Clover!

The Song of
the Self-Heal Fairy

When little elves have cut themselves,
　　Or Mouse has hurt her tail,
Or Froggie's arm has come to harm,
　　This herb will never fail.
The Fairy's skill can cure each ill
　　And soothe the sorest pain;
She'll bathe, and bind, and soon they'll find
　　That they are well again.

(This plant was a famous herb of healing in old days,
as you can tell by the names it was given—Self-Heal,
All-Heal, and others. It is also called Prunella.)

The Song of
the Stork's-Bill Fairy

"Good morning, Mr Grasshopper!
  Please stay and talk a bit!"
"Why yes, you pretty Fairy;
  Upon this grass I'll sit.
And let us ask some riddles;
  They're better fun than chat:
Why am I like the Stork's-bill?
  Come, can you answer that?"

"Oh no, you clever Grasshopper!
  I fear I am a dunce;
I cannot guess the answer—
  I give it up at once!"
"When children think they've caught me,
  I'm gone, with leap and hop;
And when they gather Stork's-bill,
  Why, all the petals drop!"

(The Stork's-bill gets her name from the long
seed-pod, which looks like a stork's beak or bill.
Others of her family are called Crane's-bills.)

The Song of the Sow Thistle Fairy

I have handsome leaves, and my stalk is tall,
  And my flowers are prettily yellow;
Yet nobody thinks me nice at all:
  They think me a tiresome fellow—
    An ugly weed
    And a rogue indeed;
  For wherever I happen to spy,
    As I look around,
    That they've dug their ground,
  I say to my seeds "Go, fly!"

  And because I am found
  On the nice soft ground,
  A trespassing weed am I!

(But I have heard that Sow Thistle is good rabbit-food,
so perhaps it is not so useless as most people think.)

THE SONG OF
THE TANSY FAIRY

In busy kitchens, in olden days,
Tansy was used in a score of ways;
Chopped and pounded,
   when cooks would make
Tansy puddings and tansy cake,
Tansy posset, or tansy tea;
Physic or flavouring tansy'd be.
         People who know
         Have told me so!

That is my tale of the past; today,
Still I'm here by the King's Highway,
Where the air from the fields
   is fresh and sweet,
With my fine-cut leaves and my flowers neat.
Were ever such button-like flowers seen—
Yellow, for elfin coats of green?
         Three in a row—
         I stitch them so!

The Song of the Ribwort Plantain Fairy

Hullo, Snailey-O!
How's the world with *you*?
Put your little horns out;
Tell me how you do?
There's rain, and dust, and sunshine,
Where carts go creaking by;
You like it wet, Snailey;
I like it dry!

Hey ho, Snailey-O,
I'll whistle you a tune!
I'm merry in September
As e'er I am in June.
By any stony roadside
Wherever you may roam,
All the summer through, Snailey,
Plantain's at home!

(There are some other kinds of Plantain besides
this. The one with wide leaves, and tall spikes of
seed which canaries enjoy, is Greater Plantain.)

The Song of
the Fumitory Fairy

Given me hundreds of years ago,
My name has a meaning you shall know:
It means, in the speech of the bygone folk,
"Smoke of the Earth"—a soft green smoke!

A wonderful plant to them I seemed;
Strange indeed were the dreams they dreamed,
Partly fancy and partly true,
About "Fumiter" and the way it grew.

Where men have ploughed
   or have dug the ground,
Still, with my rosy flowers, I'm found;
Known and prized by the bygone folk
As "Smoke of the Earth" —
   a soft green smoke!

(The name "Fumitory" was "Fumiter" 300 years ago;
and long before that, "Fume Terre", which is the French
name, still, for the plant. "Fume" means "smoke",
"terre" means "earth".)

The Song of
the Horned Poppy Fairy

These are the things I love and know:
The sound of the waves, the sight of the sea;
The great wide shore when the tide is low;
Where there's salt in the air, it's home to me—
With my petals of gold—the home for me!

The waves come up and cover the sand,
Then turn at the pebbly slope of the beach;
I feel the spray of them, where I stand,
Safe and happy, beyond their reach—
With my marvellous horns—
    beyond their reach!

The Song of
the Chicory Fairy

By the white cart-road,
　Dusty and dry,
Look! there is Chicory,
　Blue as the sky!

Or, where the footpath
　Goes through the corn,
See her bright flowers,
　Each one new-born!

Though they fade quickly,
　O, have no sorrow!
There will be others
　New-born tomorrow!

(Chicory is also called Succory.)

The Song of the
Jack-go-to-Bed-at-Noon Fairy

I'll be asleep by noon!
Though bedtime comes so soon,
   I'm busy too.
Twelve puffs!—and then from sight
I shut my flowers tight;
Only by morning light
   They're seen by you.

Then, on some day of sun,
They'll open wide, each one,
   As something new!
Shepherd, who minds his flock,
Calls it a Shepherd's Clock,
Though it can't say "tick-tock"
   As others do!

(Another of Jack's names, besides Shepherd's
Clock is Goat's Beard.)

The Song of
the Agrimony Fairies

Spikes of yellow flowers,
    All along the lane;
When the petals vanish,
    Burrs of red remain.

First the spike of flowers,
    Then the spike of burrs;
Carry them like soldiers,
    Smartly, little sirs!